Being the outcast in school is never fun,
as Elisabeth knows only too well.

Nobody ever takes your side. Nobody ever defends you.

And nobody hesitates to accuse you when
a crime has been committed.

R.W. WALLACE

AUTHOR OF THE TOLOSA MYSTERY SERIES

LET THEM EAT CAKE

A YOUNG ADULT MYSTERY SHORT STORY

Let Them Eat Cake
by R.W. Wallace

Copyright © 2019 by R.W. Wallace

Copy editing by Jinxie Gervasio
Cover by the author

All characters and events in this book, other than those clearly in the public domain, are fictitious and any resemblance to real persons, living or dead, is purely coincidental.

All rights reserved. No part of this publication may be reproduced, distributed, or transmitted in any form or by any means, including photocopying, recording, or other electronic or mechanical methods, without the prior written permission of the publisher, except in the case of brief quotations embodied in critical reviews and certain other noncommercial uses permitted by copyright law. For permission requests, write to the publisher, addressed "Attention: Permissions Coordinator," at the address below.

www.rwwallace.com

ISBN: [979-10-95707-21-9]

Main category—Fiction
Other category—Mystery

First Edition

14 13 12 11 10 / 10 9 8 7 6 5 4 3 2 1

Also by R.W. Wallace

Mystery

The Tolosa Mystery Series
The Red Brick Haze (free)
The Red Brick Cellars

Ghost Detective Shorts (coming soon)
Just Desserts
Lost Friends
Family Bonds
Till Death
Common Ground

Short Stories
Hidden Horrors
Critters
Gertrude and the Trojan Horse
First Impressions
Let Them Eat Cake
Out of Sight
Two's Company

Science Fiction (short stories)
The Vanguard
Quarantine (Lollapalooza)
Common Enemies (Lollapalooza)

Adventure (short stories)
Size Matters

Urban Fantasy (short stories)
Unexpected Consequences

LET THEM EAT CAKE

Twenty-five fourteen-year-olds make a certain amount of noise, even while trying to be quiet at eight in the morning.

The class is waiting for our teacher to arrive and we've all hung our denim jackets on the hooks lining the walls, each person always using the same hook from day to day or we'd probably never figure out which jacket belongs to who. Mine is just a hint darker than the rest of them, but it's not a ploy to stand out. It's my mother's unwillingness to part with an extra fifty bucks for *just* the right color.

We've dumped our backpacks along the walls. We have Maths, Science, *and* English today, so the damn things weigh as much as a dead donkey. I smile at myself at the thought—that's one of my favorite French expressions. It always makes me imagine a dead donkey in place of my stupidly non-cool backpack.

The cool boys are pushing each other around up by the window at the end of the hall, like they always do, and I wonder what the point is, like I always do.

The uncool boys hunch over one guy's phone, probably checking out yet another new game, or better yet, the video of a guy playing a game. That one I'll never understand.

The cool girls are—wait for it—whispering, giggling, and gossiping. Okay, I'm not actually close enough to hear what they're saying, but it's a universally known fact that when you put several cool girls together, they gossip. Probably about me. Or they may be pretending I don't exist today. Too early to tell yet.

The uncool girls…well, that would be me. And I'm not a plural, just singular little me.

I'm keeping my distance, fiddling with my phone, pretending to have important stuff to check out. I'm actually just flipping back and forth through the pages of my welcome screen, watching the colors flash by. I don't even watch videos of other people doing interesting stuff because all my focus is on my peripheral vision, making sure there are no imminent threats.

Here's to hoping high school will be better.

Our teacher, Mr. Pedersen, comes through the door at the other end of the building. All the other classes have already entered their classrooms, so he's walking down an empty hallway, but Mr. Pedersen is not one to speed up for anything. He's the youngest teacher in school—I think he's twenty-six—and the girls from the other classes are *so* jealous of our teacher.

Sure, he's handsome enough and sure, he's a nice guy. But seriously, are they expecting him to be interested in them or something? I don't think saying that's never going to happen is me being pessimistic. And they don't have to sludge through his classes every day, counting the dust motes swirling around in the classroom while he explains for the hundredth time how to draw a sixty degree angle using a pair of compasses.

Seriously, I think we understood how to do that at Christmas.

But no, Marie calls him over every day, asking him to explain it to her again. As if leaning into her cloud of stifling perfume enough times is going to make the teacher fall for her.

Him dropping dead from the stench is more likely.

"All right, kids," Mr. Pedersen says as he searches his pockets for his keys. "Time to calm down."

The noise stays the same, of course.

Mr. Pedersen opens the classroom door and steps inside. I grab my backpack and my classmates do the same. The cool boys continue shoving each other, the uncool boys still stare at their phones, and Marie and her clique are exchanging knowing glances.

I'm the last one through the door. But where I can usually make a beeline for my seat in the back, today I can only see a mass of bodies and backpacks. Being short is such a blast.

"Who did this?" Mr. Pedersen's tone is…odd. Not his usual nonchalance with a hint of a smile, but something much more strained. And angry. In the almost two years he's been our teacher, he's never been angry once. Not when Marie does one of her stunts, not when Robert smashed the glass door to the cabinets in the back while playing soccer in the classroom, and not when Daniel was caught cheating on a Maths exam.

One of the guys utters an admiring, "Dude!" and another exclaims, "That's so gross."

Daniel, who's been blocking my view, spins to face me, his face completely white and his eyes wide. Without even seeing me, he runs past me to get back out in the corridor. I think I hear him throw up out there.

Despite my general dislike of being in the middle of a group, I step into the space Daniel vacated, to see what made him go green around the gills.

So much blood.

Most of the first row of desks are covered with it, and a good part of the teacher's desk, too.

Something lies sprawled on the middle desk, Marie's, and next to it stands some sort of wooden contraption. With a blade.

"It's a cat," I say stupidly. A dead cat on Marie's desk.

"No shit, Sherlock," Marie says from her position next to Mr. Pedersen.

I shoot her a withering look, but don't bother with a comeback.

"The head's on the floor." This from Robert, who's walked around the bloody mess to the far corner of the classroom. He points to the floor by the teacher's desk. "Somebody decapitated a cat." His grin goes from ear to ear.

Stupid boys.

But I realize he's right. The poor thing on Marie's desk is indeed a headless cat.

Who would do such a thing?

"Somebody *guillotined* a cat," Marie says, voice as calm as ever, her head held in that up-tilted arrogant way she has, as if she's the queen and everybody else her worthless underlings.

She's right, though. That wooden contraption? A DIY guillotine.

They'd taken a wooden crate and removed the bottom to get a rectangular base. A large cleaver was attached to a stone—probably to make sure it's heavy enough—and tied to the top of the crate. Well, it must have been attached to the top at the start, but now it stands buried in the bottom of the crate, so far in I feel certain it must also have created a dent in the desk.

A guillotine.

We'd discussed those in French class just last week. We'd all been fascinated by the morbid history of the thing, and the way it had ended the life of the eccentric Marie Antoinette. No more cake for her.

"Don't touch that!" Mr. Pedersen's voice booms through the classroom, making me jump.

Robert stops in a half-crouched position, his hand stretched out toward what I assume is the poor cat's head on the floor.

"Jesus, Robert," Mr. Pedersen fumes. "You're not three. Show some restraint."

Robert straightens, and his cheeks turn pink, but he keeps glancing to the floor. Yeah, he'll go for it again if the teacher ever turns his back.

Mr. Pedersen must have realized the same thing. "Robert, you take all the boys with you and go to the Dean's office."

The injustice on Robert's face is almost comical. "But—"

"I'm not sending *you* to the Dean's office," Mr. Pedersen says, and I swear he's holding back an eye roll. "I'm sending you to tell the Dean about this mess and to get her to contact the police."

There's a collective intake of breath.

"The police?" Marie asks. Her gaze lands quickly on the dead cat before going back to the teacher, where it has been firmly planted since the beginning of this whole debacle. "For a dead cat?"

"Yes, Marie," Mr. Pedersen replies. "The police." I swear, it's the first time I've heard him getting annoyed with her. It's kind of refreshing.

"Off you go, Robert." Mr. Pedersen makes a shooing motion. "All the boys, out. Tell the Dean, then ask her to figure out where to put you until we get this mess straightened out."

They all grumble but follow orders. I hear someone giving Daniel a hard time for throwing up in the hallway, but less than a minute later, they're out of the building.

Mr. Pedersen crosses to the spot where Robert stood earlier. A frown appears as he sees the head on the floor, but he draws a deep breath, places his hands on his hips and glares at all of us.

"All right," he says. "Who did this?"

I freeze. He thinks one of us did it? Why not the boys?

He must have read my thought on my face. "The boys didn't do it. Their acting isn't good enough to pull off a genuine reaction like that." He glances at the bloody desk. "And they'd have done it outside, in hiding somewhere. This…this was set up by someone with a theatrical streak the size of the Antarctic."

My eyes automatically go to Marie. To my surprise, she's already looking at me.

"The only place I've seen a cleaver like that," she says, "is at Elisabeth's house. Norwegians don't use knives that big."

But my Chinese mother does. I gape at her. She's blaming this on me? Well, I guess I know who did it, then. Case closed.

But everybody's looking at me now, Mr. Pedersen included.

"I didn't—" I sputter to a stop. "I wouldn't—"

"The guillotine is French," Marie says.

And my dad's French. So, of course, I'd build a guillotine to kill a cat in my classroom. Makes perfect sense.

I point at the dead cat and finally find my voice. "I did not kill that cat."

"Nobody said you did," Mr. Pedersen says. But he's still looking at me, studying my reactions. Jesus, he actually thinks I could be the culprit?

"We all know what a guillotine is," I say. "We learned about it last week."

"I know," Mr. Pedersen says.

Ah. That's why he sent the boys away, free of all suspicion. In our class, all the girls take French, and the boys take German. We're real original like that.

I've been too focused on the teacher, so I haven't realized that the other girls have moved. Suddenly, I'm standing alone in front of the bloody mess on the front desks because the other girls have flocked around Marie in front of the blackboard.

She's got her biggest admirers flanking her; Charlotte and Christine on one side, and Nina on the other. Erin and Guro stand just an extra step back—they know they still haven't passed muster to be in the inner circle. I want to sneer at them for selling out, but I have bigger fish to fry at the moment.

I feel like I'm in court, with Mr. Pedersen as the judge and Marie and her clique as the jury—who will probably need all of five seconds to declare me guilty.

I need to regroup. Look at this objectively.

I know I didn't kill that poor cat. I'm going to assume Mr. Pedersen didn't, either. He's clearly working on the assumption that one of the girls from the class did the deed—and I'm tempted to agree. Why would someone external to the class go through the trouble of setting everything up inside a locked classroom?

"The door was locked," I say to Mr. Pedersen. "None of us have the key."

Mr. Pedersen's gaze is inscrutable as silence settles.

"You did last week," he finally says, his voice soft.

I did. We all did, at some point. We'd been working in the gymnasium all day to set up for the school play, and several of us had borrowed the key from the teacher at one point or another to make a quick jaunt to the classroom to pick something up, or to bring something back.

"But you got the key back." I hate the little whine that makes its way into my voice.

"Doesn't take long to make a copy."

I wouldn't even know how to go about that, and I say as much.

Mr. Pedersen just shrugs.

"I'm not the only one who had the opportunity to make a copy," I say and point to the group of girls around Marie. "They did, too."

"I know," Mr. Pedersen says.

I hate whining and tattling, but I have to prove my innocence. "It's a set-up," I whisper.

"What was that?" Mr. Pedersen asks. "Speak up, Elisabeth."

"They set me up," I say, my voice stronger.

"Who did?"

I point at the girls, my finger shaking, damn it. "Them. They've been after me for months, and I don't even know why."

I clear my throat and try to soldier on, but I've actually lost my train of thought.

I used to be friends with Marie and the rest of them. Then one day, I was out in the cold. No explanation, no angry words. Just silence, upturned noses, and deliberate slights throughout the day. At first, I'd tagged along, assuming everything would go back to normal.

An afternoon of insults yelled across the schoolyard for everyone to hear put a stop to that. I became a loner instead.

I've gotten used to their little games, but this is taking things too far. I'm just glad I don't have a cat, or I'm sure it would have been my animal lying there in a puddle of blood.

"Whose cat is that, anyway?" I ask. There are stray cats in the neighborhood, but the fur that's not covered in blood seems well-groomed, and I'd say it's well fed. Was.

All eyes go to the poor beast.

"Wait…" Charlotte takes a step forward, her perfectly plucked eyebrows drawn together. "Is that…?" She steps around the teacher's desk to get a look at the head.

"Kevin!" Her scream makes me jump back a step.

She's named her cat Kevin?

"You killed Charlotte's cat?" Marie moves to put her arms around her friend and pats her head as she sobs into her shoulder. "How could you?"

"I didn't kill her cat!" I'm screaming even louder than Charlotte, as if the one screaming the loudest will be believed.

Charlotte pulls a tear-and-mascara streaked face from Marie's shoulder long enough to add her two cents. "What did Kevin ever do to you? It's no wonder you have no friends. You're a freak and a monster!"

"That's enough." Mr. Pedersen's calm and adult voice makes us all take a collective deep breath. "Charlotte," he says and puts a hand on her shoulder. "Why don't you and Christine go and wait in the hallway? I'll make sure you can bring Kevin home for a proper funeral once we're done here, all right?"

Hiccupping with every step, Charlotte follows Mr. Pedersen's suggestion. Christine doesn't seem too happy with leaving her queen behind, but Marie gives a regal nod, and the two girls close the door behind them.

Erin and Guro are holding hands, their fingers clutching each other so tightly their knuckles are white. Erin's gaze is fixed on the dead cat and I'd say she's well on her way into shock. She looked much the same when she'd caught her own foot on a fishing hook last summer and had to go to the ER to get it removed.

Guro stares daggers at me. We used to be friends. I'm floored to realize she believes Marie's story over mine. She actually thinks I'm capable of killing a cat—with a bloody guillotine!—just to…I don't even know what my motive is supposed to be, honestly.

"She did this to get back at us for standing up against her," Marie says to Mr. Pedersen.

Oh, for crying out… Fine, that could make some sense, if someone believes her entire narrative.

"You're not the one standing up to me," I say as tears threaten to fall. "I'm the one who's all alone because you decided to freeze me out."

One tear escapes and makes a straight line for my jaw.

I'm so pissed right now. Not only have they made my life miserable over the last few months, but on top of that, they're forcing me to show how much it has hurt? *And* I need to convince Mr. Pedersen that I'm not a cat-killer.

I decide to face off against him instead. I'm never going to win against Marie, but at least I can make sure my teacher believes me.

"I've been completely excluded from everything since October," I say. "Yes, that makes me angry—"

"I know," Mr. Pedersen says.

"You know…?"

"I know you've not been hanging out with the other girls for a while, Elisabeth."

He knew? He knew I'd been miserable and did nothing?

I'd actually played with the idea of talking to him about my troubles. It's what they tell you to do—if you're being bullied, go to the teachers and they'll help. I hadn't been convinced by this, and it turns out my doubts had been well founded.

He knew and had just let Marie do her thing.

I feel myself deflate. My shoulders hunch and my arms cross over my chest. A year and a half before high school. Might as well be a hundred.

"What I don't know," Mr. Pedersen says, "is whether that was your choice or theirs."

"It was definitely hers, Mr. Pedersen," Marie says, her voice earnest.

God, I hate her fake ass.

She isn't done. "I sincerely hope that the murderer will be severely punished. Charlotte loved that cat like a sibling."

"Rest assured," Mr. Pedersen says with a sigh. "The culprit will be punished. But we need to figure out who did it first."

"It was her!" Marie raises her voice for the first time and points her manicured finger at me. "There can be no doubt about it, Mr. Pedersen. She killed the cat to get back at me and my friends."

"Get back for what?" Mr. Pedersen's voice is silky smooth.

I hold my breath.

"I don't know!" Marie wails. "I don't know why she hates us, I just know that she does."

Damn her for being so convincing. And for using my arguments, which would make me look like a copycat. If she can fake the feeling this easily, it means she understands perfectly what she's making me go through. Somehow, that makes everything ten times worse.

My eyes fall to the scene of the crime in front of me. I just can't look at Marie anymore, and I don't want to risk seeing accusation in Mr. Pedersen's eyes.

The guillotine looks so morbid. It had sounded weird and exciting when we'd talked about it in French class, but here, with the blade gleaming and the blood glistening, it's just gruesome. Thank God we have no death penalty in Norway, nor in France for that matter.

The wooden crate is a little out of place. It looks like one of those boxes my parents sometimes use to store jars of jam and pickled fruits. In fact…

I step closer and lean in to study the lower corner of the crate.

"What are you doing?" Marie says. "Mr. Pedersen, she's trying to tamper with the evidence."

I ignore her. I'm not planning on touching anything.

"The crate says Thorholm Fishing," I say.

I'm met with silence, so I look up. Mr. Pedersen is frowning at the crate. Marie is frowning at Mr. Pedersen. Nina has her eyes on her queen, waiting for orders—do these girls seriously have no self-respect?—and Guro and Erin are still trying to maim each other's hands. The two wannabe subjects exchange glances and I get a queasy feeling in my stomach.

I've seen this logo before. In fact, I've seen crates like these before.

"I must be getting old," Mr. Pedersen says, his eyes still on the crate. "My memory is failing me. Tell me, Erin, where does your father work again?"

Erin's basement. That's where I've seen the crates. Her father owns the factory down on the docks and brings home the crates so his wife can fill the garage with homemade jam.

"I didn't…" Erin's voice is close to a squeak.

"Is that crate from your home, Erin?" Mr. Pedersen asks.

She doesn't speak, but the tears streaking down her face are answer enough. She's still holding Guro's hand and her friend has started crying, too.

I try to picture Erin setting up the guillotine. Getting the cat. Convincing the cat to stay still while she lets the blade fall?

"You didn't do it alone," I say. "You'd need to be at least two to hold the animal in place or there's no way you'd get such a clean kill."

"Oh my God," Marie suddenly says. "I can't believe you killed Charlotte's cat! We invite you to be friends with us and this is how you repay us?"

I'm having trouble keeping up. I'm still stuck on my old friends becoming cat killers. And now Marie has turned her back on me for the first time since she accused me of being behind the cat murder and is laying into her so-called friends.

For Erin, it's the last straw. She goes from silently crying to outright bawling. I don't understand what she's trying to say, but I think "sorry" is every third word or so, and she even says my name.

What did I have to do with anything? I didn't do it, it's not my cat, I'm not the one to get decapitated.

I glance back to Mr. Pedersen. He's the teacher, the adult, shouldn't he be doing something?

His eyes are on Marie while she has her back turned. His expression is so far from his usually easygoing manner that I'm wondering if it's still the same guy. His face is drawn into hard lines and I can see the muscles of his jaw working—he must be grinding his teeth together. His eyes are laser sharp and I think his breathing is quicker than usual.

But he doesn't say anything.

Marie continues her show, with Nina as first violin. "Seriously," she says, "you think you know someone and then, bam! They go and kill your god-damned cat. What did Kevin ever do to you? I hope they expel you for this, I really do. I hope I'll never have to see your ugly mugs ever again."

Erin is still inconsolable and incomprehensible, but Guro finally speaks up. "But you told us to—"

"Oh, oh, oh!" Marie is screaming now. "I told you to what? Are you seriously going to blame this on me? What were you going to say? That I'd told you to kidnap Kevin and have him executed in our classroom? Seriously? You think anyone's going to buy that?

"If I told you to murder the Dean, would you do *that*? You do have minds of your own, don't you? You can't think for yourselves? Seriously, you expect me to *think* for you? You have to do *some* things for yourselves."

"But…but…" Guro doesn't get any further before she collapses into the arms of Erin and the two of them sink to the floor in a heap of arms, hair, tears, and hiccups.

"All right, Marie," Mr. Pedersen says. "That's enough."

"Mr. Pedersen." Marie manages a look so haughty I'm actually reminded of a painting of Marie Antoinette we'd studied in French class. "I hope they will be adequately punished for their crime."

"Marie, enough." His voice is calm, but even Marie catches the undercurrent of anger.

She shuts up.

"Marie, Nina, why don't you go join your friends in the hallway and bring them with you to the Dean's office. Tell the Dean I need her to occupy the class at least until lunch."

With a regal nod, Marie grabs Nina by the elbow and exits the room.

Why didn't he send me out, too?

I look to Mr. Pedersen for clues, but his focus is on the heap of crying teenagers on the floor. He still looks hard and angry, but his stance has turned into something more reluctant.

I take a tentative step toward the door. "Can I…?"

"Guess you're off the hook this time," he says.

"Who, me?"

"Yes, you." He sighs and nods his head toward Erin and Guro. "Those two aren't, so…"

I just stare at him.

"You do realize this was just her backup plan?" His gaze lands on the dead cat, but I'm not sure he's actually seeing it. "You were her primary target, but if she couldn't make it stick, those two would just have to do."

God, it makes so much sense.

What have I ever done to deserve such hate? She'd kill her best friend's cat to get me? To get pretty much *anyone*? Would she have thrown Nina or Charlotte to the wolves, too, if she had the chance?

"You have to stop her," I tell my teacher. "Please tell me she'll get expelled for this. Or at least suspended."

Mr. Pedersen hangs his head. "She didn't actually do anything."

"Yes, she did!"

He waves a hand to indicate the girls crying on the floor. "These two will confess as soon as they're coherent. I'm sure they'll tell us how Marie manipulated them, but I'm equally sure Marie and the rest of her clique will deny it." He runs both hands through his hair and pulls it in frustration. "And she's right, dammit. Why couldn't they think for themselves? They were the ones to actually do the deed."

My mouth is working, but no sound is coming out.

"Go join the rest of the class in the administrative building, will you?" Even though he's talking to me, his eyes are on Erin and Guro. "And stay away from Marie."

Let Them Eat Cake

༶

The cool boys are still shoving at each other and the uncool boys are still hunched over their phones. The cool girls are still gossiping and I'm still on high alert.

The seat at the back of the class is still mine, and I'm still counting dust motes.

But we're not drawing sixty-degree angles anymore. Mr. Pedersen doesn't lean over Marie's desk to show her things when she asks questions. He stays at the blackboard.

The two seats in front of mine, where Erin and Guro used to sit, are empty.

And Charlotte has changed seats, from the one next to Marie to the one on my left. So far, we've only exchanged hellos, but I'm confident we'll get there.

One down, the rest of the class to go.

We'll get there.

THANK YOU

THANK YOU FOR reading *Let Them Eat Cake.* I hope you enjoyed it!

If you liked the it, you might want to check out some of my other books mentioned on the next page. It's mostly Mysteries, but a few Science Fiction short stories will pop up, too.

And don't forget that the first book of my *Tolosa Mystery* series, *The Red Brick Haze*, is available for free on my website.

R.W. Wallace
www.rwwallace.com

Also by R.W. Wallace

Mystery

THE TOLOSA MYSTERY SERIES
The Red Brick Haze (free)
The Red Brick Cellars

GHOST DETECTIVE SHORTS (COMING SOON)
Just Desserts
Lost Friends
Family Bonds
Till Death
Common Ground

SHORT STORIES
Hidden Horrors
Critters
Gertrude and the Trojan Horse
First Impressions
Let Them Eat Cake
Out of Sight
Two's Company

Science Fiction (short stories)
The Vanguard
Quarantine (Lollapalooza)
Common Enemies (Lollapalooza)

Adventure (short stories)
Size Matters

Urban Fantasy (short stories)
Unexpected Consequences

www.ingramcontent.com/pod-product-compliance
Lightning Source LLC
LaVergne TN
LVHW041603070526
838199LV00047B/2123